BLUE BUG'S
Vegetable Garden

By Virginia Poulet

Illustrated by Donald Charles

CHILDRENS PRESS, CHICAGO

For William and Mary Sowinski,
my father and mother

C. 3

Library of Congress Cataloging in Publication Data

Poulet, Virginia.
  Blue Bug's vegetable garden.

  SUMMARY: Blue Bug encounters many vegetables
while searching for his favorite one.
  [1. Vegetables—Stories. 2. Space perception—
Fiction] I. Charles, Donald, illus. II. Title.
PZ10.3.P484Bq   [E]   73-8896
ISBN 0-516-03421-9

XJ
POULET

19 20 21 22 R 93 92

BLUE BUG'S
Vegetable Garden

4

Blue Bug
looked high

7

up

9

10

down

over

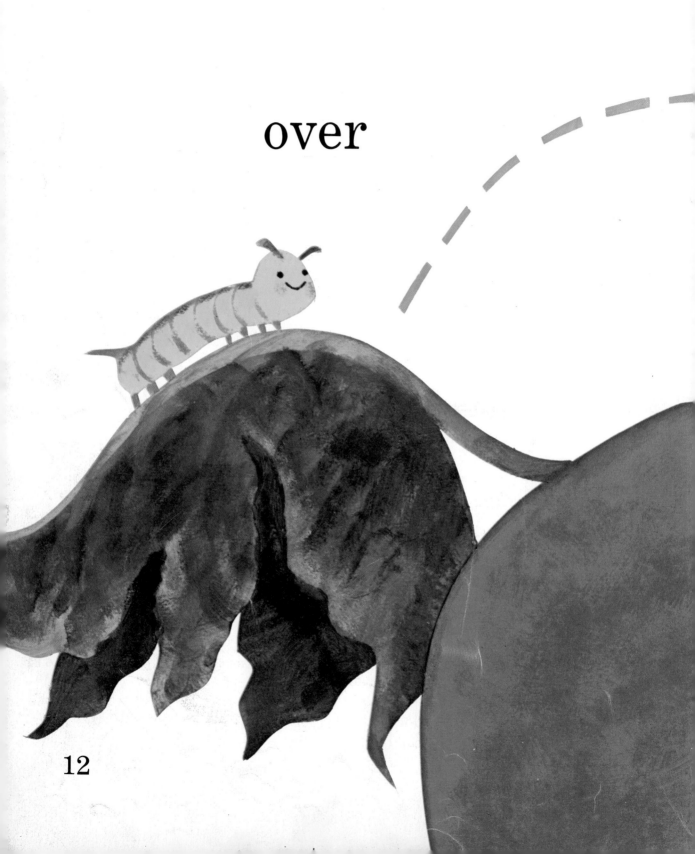

12

13

under

around

17

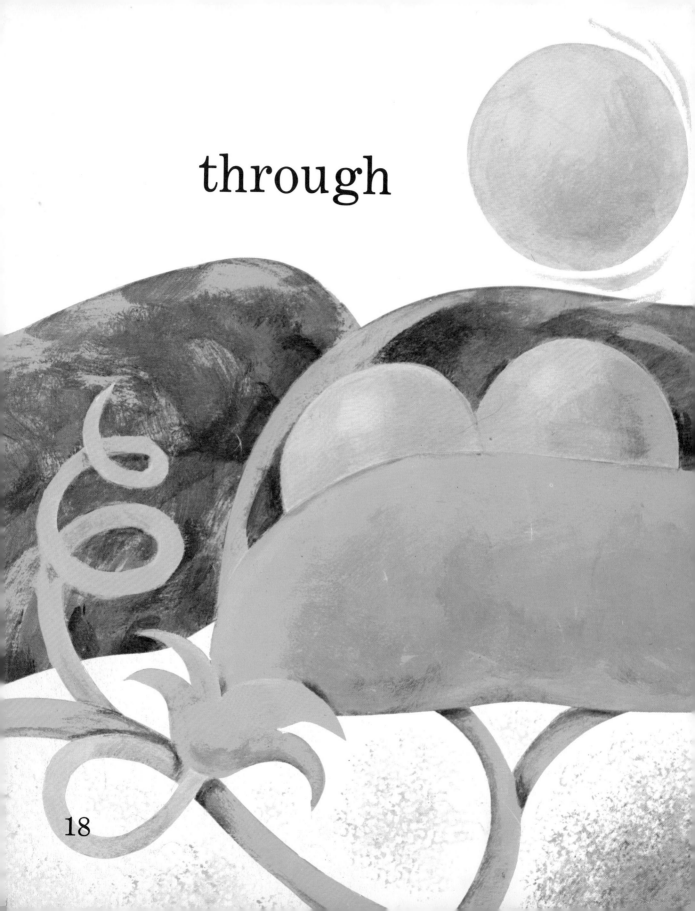

through

18

19

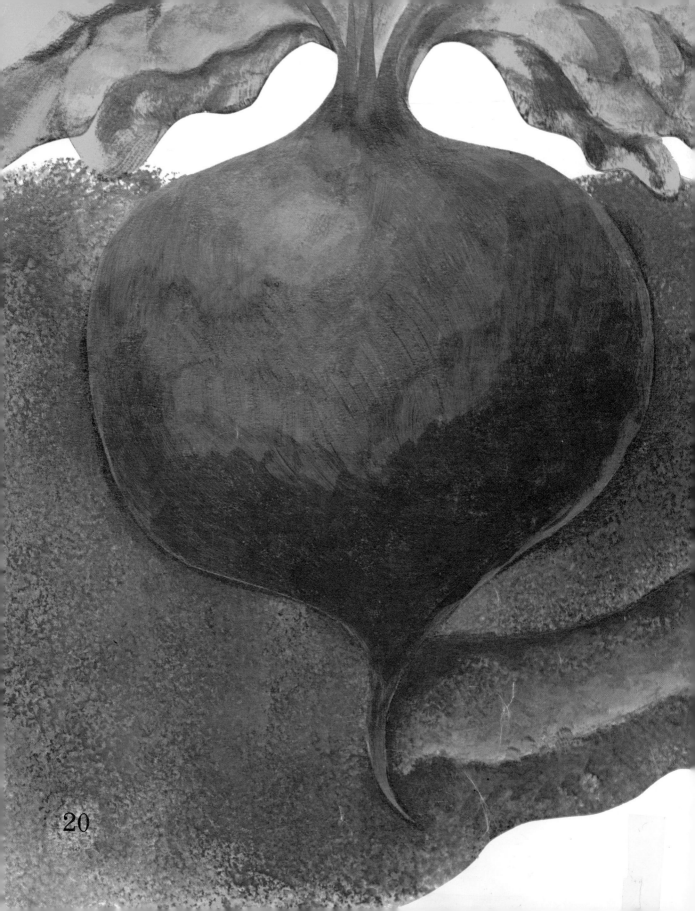

20

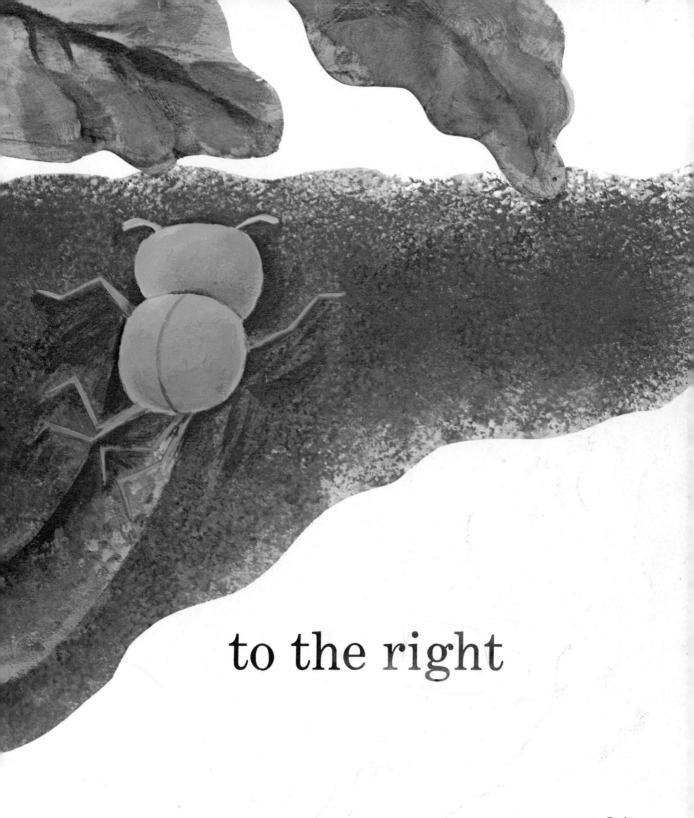

to the right

to the left

and in the dark

to find his
favorite food...

28

... ONIONS!

How does your favorite vegetable grow?

The Sunshine Vegetables

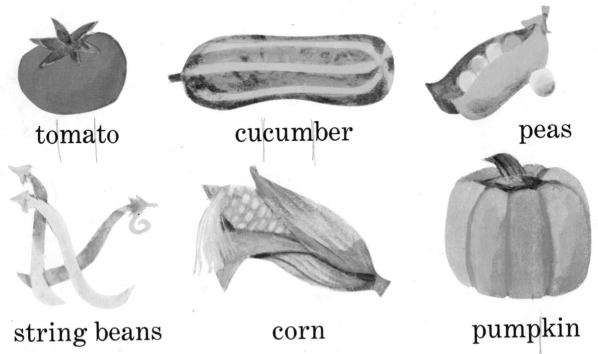

tomato   cucumber   peas

string beans   corn   pumpkin

The Underground Vegetables

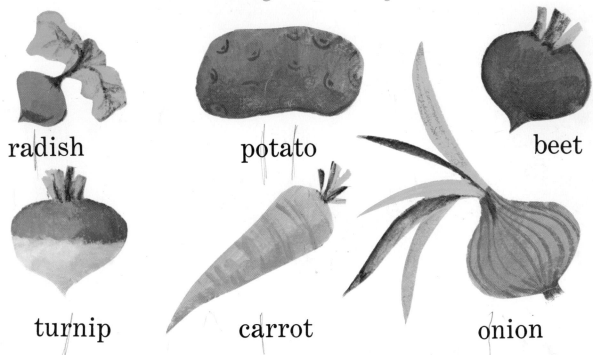

radish   potato   beet

turnip   carrot   onion

31

About the Author: Virginia Maniglier-Poulet lives with her husband and two young children in Tulsa, Oklahoma. After graduating as a fashion design major from Washington University in St. Louis, she designed women's lingerie for a year, then served in the Peace Corps in Morocco for two years. Recognizing a definite need for very simple, yet stimulating beginning readers, she developed her first book, *Blue Bug and the Bullies.* She feels that the illustration should catch the child's interest and stimulate him to try to actually READ the WORD, not read the picture. Her children's criticisms were pertinent to the development of *Blue Bug and the Bullies* and *Blue Bug's Safety Book,* as well as *Blue Bug's Vegetable Garden.*

About the Artist: Donald Charles started his long career as an artist more than twenty-five years ago after attending the University of California and the Art League School of California. He began by writing and illustrating feature articles for the San Francisco Chronicle, and also sold cartoons and ideas to The New Yorker and Cosmopolitan magazines. Since then he has been, at various times, a longshoreman, ranch hand, truck driver, and editor of a weekly newspaper, all enriching experiences for an artist. Ultimately he became creative director for an advertising agency, a post which he resigned several years ago to devote himself full-time to book illustration and writing. Mr. Charles has received frequent awards from graphic societies, and his work has appeared in numerous textbooks and periodicals. He and his artist wife have restored a turn-of-the-century frame house in Chicago where they live with their three children.